T0374093

Flash Visits Outer Space

By Charlie Alexander

Copyright © 2016 by Charlie Alexander. 747384
Library of Congress Control Number: 2016912513

ISBN: Softcover   978-1-5245-2994-9
        Hardcover   978-1-5245-2995-6
        EBook   978-1-5245-2993-2

All rights reserved. No part of this book may
be reproduced or transmitted in any form or by
any means, electronic or mechanical, including
photocopying, recording, or by any information storage
and retrieval system, without permission in writing from
the copyright owner.

This is a work of fiction. Names, characters,
places and incidents either are the product of the
author's imagination or are used fictitiously, and any
resemblance to any actual persons, living or dead,
events, or locales is entirely coincidental.

Print information available on the last page.

Rev. date: 8/3/2016

To order additional copies of this book, contact:
Xlibris
1-888-795-4274
www.Xlibris.com
Orders@Xlibris.com

Flash Visits Outer Space

Written by Charlie Alexander
Art Work by Charlie Alexander

The jets were transporting Flash and the other astronauts to the launch pad.

Here they come

Lift off in twenty two hours.

The astronauts were being driven to the shuttle.

It was almost time.

"5 4 3 2 1 ...we have lift off!" cheered Flash.

The rumble of the engines filled the air!

"I can see the earth and moon and the sun."

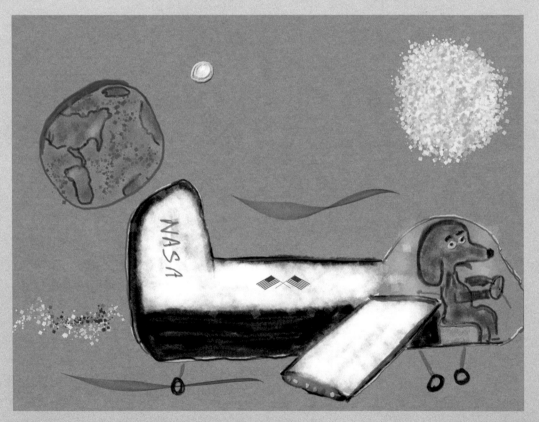

Flying the shuttle was a big responsibility.

"There's the space station!" declared Flash.

It was bigger than Flash expected.

"I'm passing through a solar flair!" Flash said very quickly.

"I hope we make it!" Flash waived
to the sun as he passed by.

"There really are rings around Saturn."

Flash was thrilled to be circling just like the rings.

"There's the space station again!" said Flash.

"That's where we'll sleep tonight."
Flash said with a yawn.

"This way to Mars!"

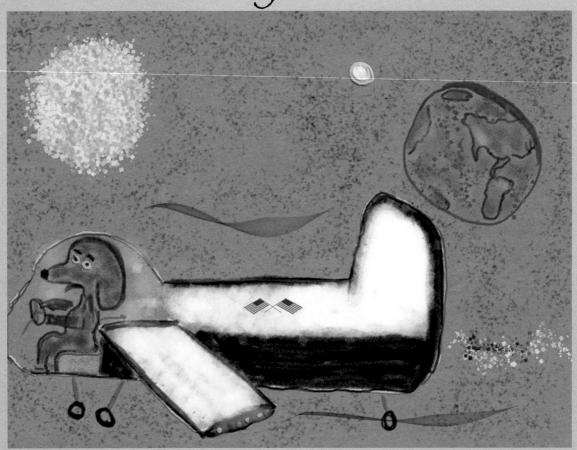

Flash was going where no poodle
had ever gone before!

"Payload has been delivered!"

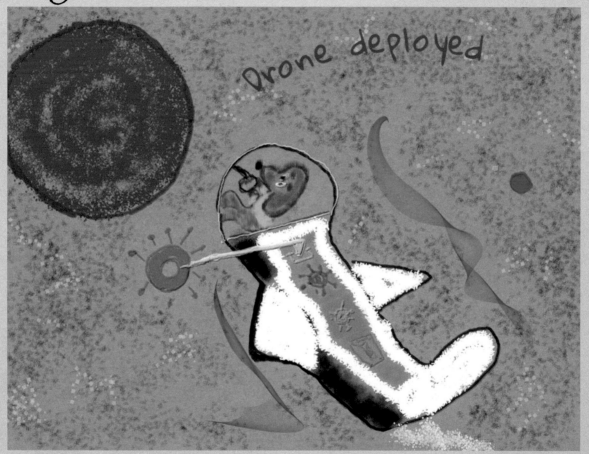

"Mars really does look red!" thought Flash.

"I love trying to fly with a comet!" Flash snickered.

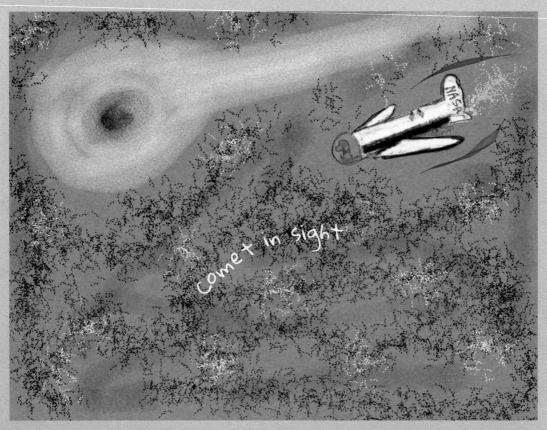

"We sure are going fast!"

"Good day for a space walk."

Flash was dressed in his space suit.

Flash had to figure out which satellite needed the repair.

"I think it's the one going behind the earth right now." observed Flash.

Moon rocket in flight!

Hold on Flash!

As Flash was zipping past the moon...

Flash thought he saw a mouse sitting on the edge of the moon. "I think he was crying." reported Flash.

"And the cow jumped over the moon." stated Flash.

The three astronauts thought the cow would never make it! But she did!

Flash had the best view of the eclipse.

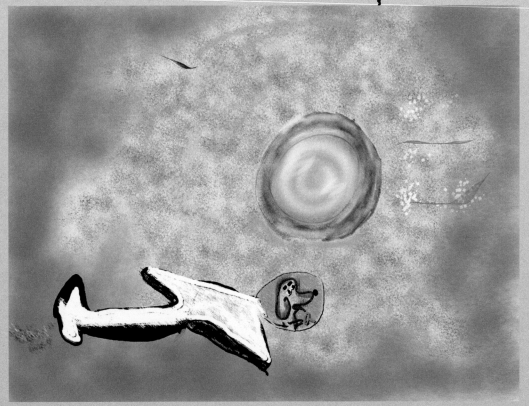

"Is that a solar or lunar eclipse?" he asked.

Flash wondered who or what he might meet.

Would he actually visit an alien?

"All the space you could ever want!"

It made Flash feel a little small.

Flash had a dream that he was Santa flying through space!

"On dancer and prancer! Lead the way Rudolph!"

All of a sudden, Flash saw a UFO.

It looked like a flying saucer.

And just as quickly, it disappeared into the dark vastness.

Flash tried to catch up with it!

Even though Flash opened the engines full...

His new friend was out of sight in an instant.

Flash looked at his fuel gauge and knew it was time to head home.

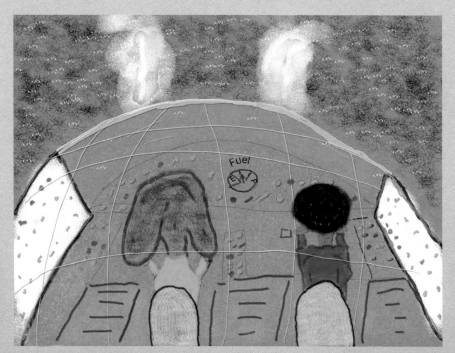

He was anxious to see everyone back on earth.

"I'm almost home! I can't wait to see Charlie and Becky!"

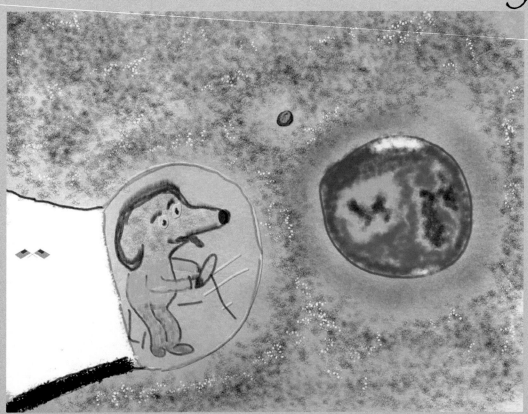

It was time for Flash to start his orbit.

"I'm about to begin orbit for final descent!"

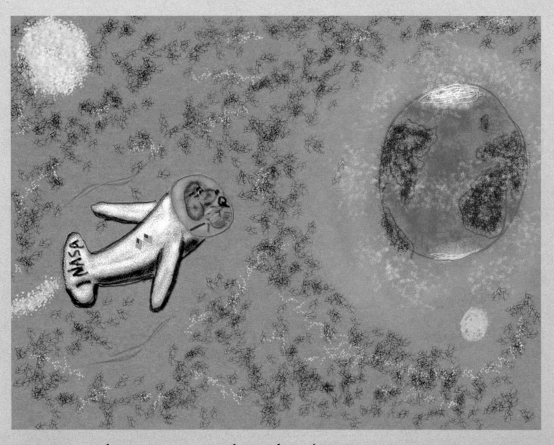

It was good to be home again!

"The capsule has landed safely!" signaled Flash.

"There's not much room in there!"

Time to get a medical checkup.

And then onto enjoy a celebration with friends!

Flash and the other astronauts passed their medical tests.

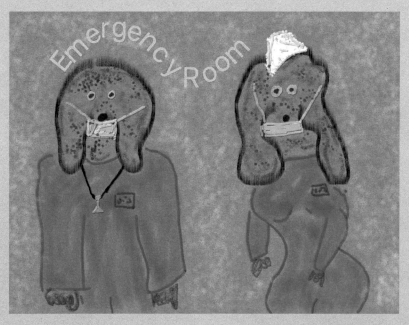

"Now for some goodies and a chance to stretch our legs." Flash said, as he took a bite of a cookie.

The party was at Charlie and Becky's house.

It had all been planned weeks ago!

"Home at last!
There's no place like home."

"Especially at lunch time!" laughed Flash!

The End

Printed in the United States
By Bookmasters